'S

DONALD DUCK

Luck of the

DUCKS!

chess is a

BIG Gorgius

Gorgiaus

STOP

Girl's
FERRY

WALT DISNEY'S

DONALD DUCK
LUCK OF THE DUCKS

by
Carl Fallberg

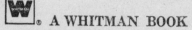 A WHITMAN BOOK

Western Publishing Company, Inc.
Racine, Wisconsin

CONTENTS

Sweet Dreams

CHAPTER 1

FALSE ALARM

It was a dark and stormy night in Duckburg. Lightning flashed, thunder rumbled, and a driving, windswept rain lashed at Donald's house.

Inside, however, Donald and his nephews slept soundly in their cozy beds, stirring only occasionally as a thunderclap rattled the windows.

Down the deserted street came a car. It skidded to a stop in front of Donald's house. A spotlight played over the front door, resting for a moment on the house number. Then a man dressed in rain gear got out of the car and hurried up the walk.

He pressed the doorbell. Getting no response, he banged on the door with his fist.

In a moment a sleepy Donald, wearing one slipper and with a

An Unknown Visitor

robe half over his nightshirt, came
downstairs grumpily and opened
the door.

"Donald Duck?" asked the drip-
ping stranger, shoving a damp envelope and a pencil and paper at
Donald. "Airmail, special delivery,
certified, registered, insured, return receipt requested! Sign here!"

Donald did so. Then he took the
envelope and closed the door. At
that moment his three nephews
came trooping down the stairs.

"What was it?" asked Huey.

"Sign Here!"

"Oh, nothing!" answered Donald with a yawn. "Just an airmail, special delivery, certified, registered, insured, return receipt requested letter!"

"Gosh!" said Dewey, wide-eyed. "It sounds important! Aren't you going to open it?"

"Yeah, guess I might as well," mumbled Donald. He tore open the envelope and tossed it aside.

" 'Dear sir!' " he read. " 'We are happy to inform you that you have won first prize of ten thousand

A Message for Donald

dollars cash in our super, terrific, colossal Treasure Trove contest, you lucky fellow you! Please bring your entry blank receipt to our office within five days to claim your prize!' Signed, 'Bubblesy Wubblesy Soap Company'!"

Donald dropped the letter and started up the stairs. "Imagine waking me up in the middle of the night just for that junk mail!" he grumbled. Then, halfway up, he stopped cold as the realization of what he had read hit him.

A Startled Winner

"TEN THOUSAND DOL-LARS!" he cried. He flew down the steps, grabbed the letter, and read it again. He was quite wide-awake now. "Pinch me, somebody!" he exclaimed.

The kids obliged. "Ouch!" yelled Donald. "Don't overdo it!"

"Did you enter a contest for the Bubblesy Wubblesy Soap Company?" asked Huey.

Donald pondered a moment. "Yeah, I think so," he answered. "Couple of months ago! It was one

"TEN THOUSAND DOLLARS!"

of those deals where they were in-
troducing a new bubble bath or
something."

"I remember that!" said Louie.
"You took so many baths the whole
house was full of bubbles for a
week. You were the cleanest duck
in all Duckburg, I'll bet!"

"Never mind, comedian," replied
Donald archly. "Who's got the last
laugh now?"

"By the way, Unca Donald," put
in Huey, "do you still have your
entry blank receipt?"

"Never Mind, Comedian."

Donald blinked. "Golly, I think so. It's probably in my desk."

He raced over to the desk and began digging frantically through drawers, throwing papers all over the place.

"Not in here," he muttered. "It may be stuck in a book." He began pulling books and magazines off the shelves and flipping through them. Soon the room was a shambles of reading matter.

Huey, meanwhile, had picked up the envelope. Suddenly his eyes

A Frantic Search

popped. "Unca Donald!" he gasped.
"Look at this!"

"Don't bother me. I'm busy,"
his uncle snapped as he started for
the kitchen. "Maybe I put it in the
refrigerator or someplace."

Huey blocked his way. "But,
Unca Donald," he persisted. "It's
kind of important."

"Oh, all right!" said Donald in
exasperation. "What is it?"

"Better sit down first," replied
Huey. He shoved a chair behind his
frowning uncle. Donald obeyed

"Look at This!"

with an impatient sigh.

"Okay, what's so important?"

Huey gulped. "Th-this letter isn't for you. It's for *Gladstone Gander!*"

Donald turned pale—as pale as a duck can get. "Gladstone Gander?" he repeated. "Let me see that." He grabbed the envelope and stared at it in disbelief.

"Oh, no!" he groaned. "Not my deadbeat, mooching cousin!"

"Your fantastically lucky, deadbeat, mooching cousin," corrected

A Dreadful Mistake

Huey. "Looks like he did it again."

Donald sat stunned, a blank look on his face. "Why Gladstone?" he muttered. "Hasn't he won enough contests already? Can't he *ever* lose?"

The kids shook their heads sympathetically. Through the years Gladstone's fantastic luck had been a source of wonder and irritation to Donald. And while it didn't bother the kids, their envious uncle took it to heart. Gladstone seemed to be born under the sign of a four-

"Why Gladstone?"

leaf clover, for he had never had to work a day in his life.

"C'mon, Unca Donald, let's go to bed and get some sleep," urged Huey.

Donald crumpled the envelope and threw it away. "Okay," he sighed, "but I don't feel like sleeping. I wonder why in blazes Gladstone had that letter sent here. Maybe just to bug me. I wouldn't put it past him."

Muttering sadly to himself, he followed the boys up the stairs.

"Let's Get Some Sleep."

A Nasty Nightmare

CHAPTER 2

A CHANGE OF LUCK

Needless to say, Donald slept somewhat fitfully the rest of the night. He had nightmares about chasing money which would blow away just as he was about to grab it.

When morning finally came, Donald awoke to find that the

storm had let up a bit. He dragged
himself out of bed and went downstairs to find the kids already up.
They knew better than to comment
on the night's activities. An awk-
ward silence was broken by the
doorbell's ring.

"It better not be another prize for
Gladstone!" growled Donald as he
opened the door.

It was worse than that. It was
Gladstone Gander himself, smiling
happily in the morning gloom.

"Morning, cuz," he said breezily

"Morning, Cuz!"

as he strode in past Donald. "Mind if I come in?"

"What choice have I got?" Donald muttered, closing the door. Gladstone turned and peered at him.

"You look awful!" he observed, settling himself down in an easy chair. "Have a bad night? Uh, by the way, is there any mail for me?"

Donald turned beet-red. He was about to shout an angry "NO!" when helpful Huey came in with the prize letter.

"This came for you, Gladstone,"

"You Look Awful!"

he said. "We opened it by mistake."

Gladstone read it quickly. "Hmm, I was expecting that," he remarked casually.

Then Donald found his voice. Why, he demanded angrily, was Gladstone's mail sent here in the middle of the night?

Gladstone calmly explained that he had been winning so many contests that people had begun pestering him for money. Therefore, he had decided to change his address.

"Matter of fact," he continued,

Gladstone Gets a Scolding

"I'm looking around for a nice, quiet house. I was wondering if you'd mind if I. . . ."

"No!" yelled Donald, reading his mind. "We're overcrowded the way it is."

"Okay, okay," said Gladstone as he started for the door. "I just thought I'd ask. Guess I'll mosey down and collect my prize money." He paused at the door. "Uh, which contest was that again? Bubblesy Wubblesy or Crackley Wackley?"

He stepped out. Suddenly he

"Okay, Okay."

whipped back in and slammed the door, a frightened expression on his face.

"It—it's that car again!" he whispered hoarsely, sweat beading his brow.

"What car?" asked Donald suspiciously, looking out the window. The rainswept street was empty except for Gladstone's sports car at the curb. "All I see is that souped-up job of yours."

Gladstone peeked out. "B-But it was there a second ago! A big black

"It's That Car Again!"

sedan with a couple of guys in it. It's been following me for days!"

"Huh!" snorted Donald. "Probably a bill collector. Besides, what're you worried about? With your luck, nothing could happen to you."

Gladstone pleaded to be allowed to stay for a few days. Donald was firm in his refusal; he thought it was just another one of Gladstone's deadbeat tricks.

"Aw, let him stay!" urged Huey. "He's kinda fun, and, besides, some

"Aw, Let Him Stay!"

of his luck might rub off on you, Unca Donald!"

"Sure, cuz," added Gladstone. "You could use some!"

Before Donald could think of a nasty retort, there was a blinding flash of lightning outside, accompanied by a clap of thunder that shook the house.

"Wow!" cried Louie. "Sounded like it hit right in our front yard!"

They crowded to the window and looked out. Sure enough, lightning had struck an old tree by the curb,

A Disastrous Sight

shattering it to pieces. A thin plume
of smoke was rising from a ragged,
gaping hole in the roof of Gladstone's car.

"Smoley hokes!" gasped Dewey.
"It hit Gladstone's car, too!"

The ducks dashed outside to view
the destruction. They found that
there was also a scorched hole the
size of a basketball in the seat of
the car.

"Too bad about your car, cuz,"
said Donald, trying hard to sound
sympathetic.

"Too Bad About Your Car."

Gladstone was speechless for a change. He just stared at his car, stunned by the catastrophe.

"Gee, Unca Donald," said Huey, examining the shattered tree, "the lightning split this ol' tree up into pieces just the right size for our fireplace!"

"Maybe some of Gladstone's luck is rubbing off on you," observed Dewey.

Donald just grunted. Then, with a slightly smug smile, he generously offered to drive his unlucky cousin

Speechless Onlookers

down to collect his prize.

Gladstone said nothing. Instead, he went back into the house to brood. The kids started lugging the firewood around to the backyard, and Donald examined the car more closely.

A big black car containing two men pulled up to the curb, and the driver, a beefy fellow in a turtle-neck sweater, got out.

"Tough luck, bud," he remarked. "Your car?"

"Nope," answered Donald. "It

"Tough Luck, Bud."

belongs to my lucky cousin."

The man rubbed his stubbly chin thoughtfully. "What do you mean, *lucky* cousin?"

Donald couldn't resist the chance to put down Gladstone even further. He told the man about his cousin's incredible luck, and how he always came up smelling like a rose—till now.

Turtleneck peered into the car. "Well," he said, "seems like your cousin's luck still holds—and then some!"

"Lucky Cousin?"

A Startling Discovery

CHAPTER 3

DUCKNAPPED!

"What do you mean?" asked Donald.

"Look," replied the man, pointing to the hole in the front seat. "It wasn't lightning that hit the car. It was a meteorite!"

Donald stared down at the hole. He saw a smoking chunk of rock resting on the pavement. It seemed to glow and sparkle with life!

"Looks like it's full of gems, too," continued Turtleneck. "Worth a fortune, probably."

Then the other man in the car, a grizzled old fellow with a face like a dried prune, spoke up. "Huh," he remarked sourly. "We should have bad luck like that."

Turtleneck turned to his companion. "Don't worry, Feisty," he said. "I've got a feeling our luck is going to change from now on!"

A Valuable Find

He then asked Donald if they could meet his famous cousin. He explained that they were a couple of reporters doing a series of stories on people with interesting relatives, and that they would like very much to interview Donald and take some pictures.

Donald, of course, was flattered. He agreed enthusiastically. "This way, gentlemen!" he said eagerly, leading the way to the house and through the front door.

Inside, Gladstone was still and

"This Way, Gentlemen!"

brooding, trying to figure out his apparent bad luck.

"Some reporters here want to interview you, Gladstone!" announced Donald.

Gladstone looked up glumly. "Reporters?" He frowned. "You know I never give interviews unless I'm paid for it!"

Turtleneck whipped out a big, black automatic. "You're going to give this one for free!" he rasped.

Gladstone gulped, then managed a weak smile. "Er, uh, sure, if you

Turtleneck Means Business

put it that way," he faltered.

The big gunman gestured toward the door. "Out!" he barked. Then he jabbed the gun in Donald's face. "You, too!"

The two puzzled and frightened cousins started for the door. Just then the nephews burst in, bowling them over in a heap.

"Gladstone, come quick!" yelled the kids. "There's a meteorite under your car!"

They stopped short as they saw the man with the gun. "Oh, sorry!"

"Gladstone, Come Quick!"

gulped Huey. "We didn't know you had company."

They quickly started out, but Feisty slammed the door. "Hold it!" he snapped. He ripped a drape from the window and threw it over the petrified kids. "You're coming with us, too!"

He gathered the drapeful of kids into a big bag and slung it over his shoulder.

"Let's go!" he ordered, and they moved out into the rain. Gladstone gasped when he saw the black car.

"You're Coming With Us!"

"Th-that's the one that's been following me!" he stammered. Regaining a bit of his courage, he demanded to know what the big idea was.

"You'll find out soon enough," growled Turtleneck. "Get in the car before we get soaked."

Feisty and the ducks piled in the back, and Turtleneck slipped behind the wheel. In a moment they were roaring down the rain-slick street.

They were hardly under way

Worried Captives

when the wail of a siren sounded
behind them. "Cops!" exclaimed
Feisty in alarm, looking out the
rear window. Sure enough, a patrol
car with blinking red lights was
bearing down on them.

"Must be because we were
parked by a fireplug," said Turtleneck, tromping on the gas. "I'm
gonna try and outrun 'em!"

"Are you crazy?" yelled Feisty.
"We can't outrun a police car in
this heap. Our brakes are bad, and
the tires are as smooth as eggs!"

"Cops!"

"We have no choice," replied the driver grimly. "We don't dare let 'em stop us! We'd have a hard time explaining these ducks!"

The heap picked up speed, and the speedometer needle climbed steadily to 60, then 70 . . . 80 . . . 90! The police car still clung to their rear, siren screaming, as they careened wildly through the stormy streets.

The needle edged past the 100 mark. Suddenly it flew off the dash-board with a *sprong!* Still the car

Pursuing the Thieves

continued to gain speed.

"Stop!" screamed Feisty, by now a bit worried. "We must be flying low!"

"I can't," yelled Turtleneck. "The accelerator's stuck!"

Miraculously, he managed to miss traffic, trees, houses, lamp-posts, pedestrians, and buildings by a gnat's eyelash as the car streaked through the storm like an unguided missile. The siren grew fainter and fainter behind them. Finally it faded away.

A Narrow Escape

"Hey, we outran 'em!" shouted Turtleneck jubilantly as he swung the car down a deserted street and drove into the waterfront section. He applied the brakes and the car glided to a perfect stop.

Safe at Last

Pals

CHAPTER 4

UNWILLING ACCOMPLICES

"Now what do you think about our luck, Feisty?" gloated Turtle-neck.

"Well, maybe it has taken a turn for the better," admitted Feisty.

"You bet it has!" exclaimed the other, reaching back and slapping Gladstone on the back. "Thanks to

Mr. Gander here!"

Suddenly the car began to shake violently. With a great crash it collapsed into small pieces.

"Well," Feisty remarked ruefully as they picked themselves up out of the wreckage, "guess you can push even that lucky Gander's luck too far!"

Donald, who had been silent during the mad chase, spoke up. "Yeah, his luck's bound to run out sooner or later."

Gladstone bristled at this. "It has

Pushing Luck Too Far

not," he declared firmly. "You just wait and see!" If there was anything Gladstone resented, it was for someone to doubt his luck.

"He's right!" confirmed Turtleneck, who had been rummaging in the wreckage. "Look at this!" He held up a bundle of banknotes. "Here's that missing dough we thought we'd lost after our last caper. Must have been stuck under the seat!"

"See, I told you!" declared the lucky Gander smugly.

"Here's the Missing Dough."

Turtleneck slapped him on the back again. "Yes, sir, you're gonna be our little lucky ducky wucky," he enthused. "Now I can throw away my rabbit's foot and four-leaf clover and the rest of those lucky charms."

Donald still wasn't convinced. "How about *me?*" he growled. "I don't call *this* good luck."

His nephews had by now worked their way out of the bag. They affirmed their faith in Gladstone's luck.

"Our Lucky Ducky."

"Trouble is, you don't believe in Gladstone's luck, Unca Donald!" chided Huey. "We do!"

"Simple childish faith," sneered Donald. "Pure coincidence."

"Oh, yeah?" shot back Gladstone. "I'll bet I could jump off that pier and come up with a handful of pearls!"

"Wait a minute," broke in Turtleneck. "I've got a better idea. Why don't we pull off that Gotrocks Jewelry Store caper we goofed last week?" He pointed to Gladstone.

A Little Misunderstanding

"With him along, we can't lose!"

Feisty pondered a moment. "But they've got armed guards and burglar alarms and closed circuit TV all over the joint!"

Gladstone, puffed up by pride in his luck, took Turtleneck's side. "He's right!" he declared. "With me along, you can't lose!"

The kids, aghast at Gladstone's attitude, tried to plead with him to think of what he was doing.

Turtleneck shut them up. "Knock it off!" he bellowed. He looked hard

"Knock It Off!"

at Gladstone. "Your luck better
keep on working, or else you and
your relatives are gonna be in big
trouble."

The first thing the crooks had to
do was to find a getaway car. Luckily, a florist, making a delivery
nearby, had left his truck with the
motor running.

"Like on a silver platter!" said
Turtleneck happily as he and Feisty
locked the ducks in the back and
took off.

The thunderstorm had begun

The Getaway Truck

again in earnest as they pulled up in front of the jewelry store.

"Look!" exclaimed Turtleneck, beaming. "The parking meter even has some time left on it!"

Encouraged by this good omen, they quickly entered the jewelry store, holding Gladstone between them and carrying bouquets of flowers to hide their guns.

The guard at the door gave them only a passing glance. In a moment a smiling clerk approached and asked if he could be of any help.

A Big Job Ahead

Feisty replied that they were looking for a birthday gift for their dear old mother. They would like to see something nice in the way of jewelry, he said, and price was no object.

The salesman was only too happy to oblige. Soon there was a huge collection of rings, watches, bracelets, and necklaces spread on the counter.

While the man was arranging the display, Feisty glanced nervously at the guards. "If your

A Choice Display

luck's gonna work, it better start working soon!" he whispered to Gladstone.

"Don't worry," Gladstone whispered back. "It will!" He was so intent on proving his luck that he quite overlooked the seriousness of the situation.

"Have you decided, gentlemen?" asked the clerk.

"Yes!" replied Turtleneck with a hard smile. "We'll take *all* of it!" He dropped his bouquet and leveled his gun at the startled salesman.

"We'll Take All of It!"

"And don't bother to gift wrap it.
We'll just stick it in this sack!"

Feisty started stuffing the loot
into a large bag. The salesman, recovering from his initial shock,
began edging his foot toward a
burglar alarm button on the floor.
At that moment there was a blinding flash of lightning, along with
an ear-splitting crack, as a bolt hit
a high-tension line outside and
knocked out the store's power.

"That's it! Let's go!" exclaimed
Feisty as he scooped the last of the

Sounding the Alarm

loot into the bag. Turtleneck grabbed Gladstone's arm. In a few moments they were zooming off down the street—before the confused guards could gather their wits.

"Was that luck or wasn't it?" chortled Turtleneck as they wove their way through the storm. His partner in crime had to admit it certainly was.

Carried away by the success of the Gotrocks caper, the lucky bandits hit four more jewelry stores,

The Bandits Flee

three banks, and a candy store in quick succession. The loot soon piled up in the back of the truck, crowding Donald and the kids so that they could hardly move.

"There's no stopping us now, Gladstone baby!" chuckled Turtle-neck. "Who knows? Maybe next week, Fort Knox!"

A Happy Threesome

Gloomy Predicament

CHAPTER 5

ALMOST MAROONED

In the back of the truck Donald gloomed about their predicament. "If Gladstone hadn't been so blame lucky all his life, we wouldn't be in this mess," he moaned.

The kids had their own idea. "If you hadn't shot your beak off about his luck, you mean," Huey, Dewey, and Louie thought to themselves.

Aloud, Huey observed, "We have to figure out a way to get Gladstone out of this, because we sorta got him into it."

"The heck with Gladstone!" snapped Donald. "He can take care of himself! How about *us?*"

"Don't worry, Unca Donald," soothed Dewey. "Maybe some of his luck will rub off on us!"

"That'll be the day," grumped Donald, settling down in the loot to sulk.

"That'll Be the Day!"

It was sometime later that day when the truck finally came to a bumpy stop. The ducks were roused from a half-sleep.

"Wonder where we are," muttered Donald with a yawn. "Fort Knox?"

"Not unless they've moved it to the seashore," replied Huey. "I smell salt water."

"I hear sea gulls," said Dewey.

"And waves lapping," added Louie.

At that moment the rear door of

"Wonder Where We Are?"

the truck was unlocked by Turtleneck. "End of the line!" he barked.
"All out!"

The ducks climbed out stiffly to
find themselves on a stretch of
lonely, fog-swept beach. Nearby
was a rickety pier to which an ancient schooner was moored. Barely
legible on the bow was the name
Bouncing Barnacle.

"Lend a hand with that loot and
take it aboard the schooner," ordered Feisty.

"Wait a minute," balked Donald.

"All Out!"

"We've been through enough.
Carry your old loot yourself!"

In a moment he changed his mind,
as he stared into the business end
of Turtleneck's automatic. "Okay,
if you put it that way," he gulped
as he grabbed a sack of jewels.

The others reluctantly followed
suit. As they moved across the
beach Gladstone tripped over a
large oyster shell. He fell flat on
his face.

"Ohhh!" he groaned, feeling one
leg gingerly. "I think I broke a leg

Unloading the Jewels

or something. Guess my luck's finally run out."

He was putting on an act, hoping the crooks would let him go.

"Oh, yeah?" exclaimed Turtle-neck, picking up the shell which had tripped Gladstone. "Get a load of this!"

He plucked a large pearl out of the shell and held it in front of Gladstone's nose. "I think we'll keep you around for a while!" he said with a smirk.

The loot was soon stored aboard

"Get a Load of This!"

the schooner. Then Donald, naturally, wanted to know what was
going to happen to them.

"Well," answered Feisty, as he
rubbed his scraggly chin, "Mr. Gander is going on a cruise with us—
as a first-class passenger! He'll be
treated well, don't worry."

"How about us?" persisted Donald, meaning the kids and himself.

Feisty pointed to a small rocky
reef offshore. "Oh, you ducks are
due for a nice vacation because
you've worked so hard!" He smiled

Due for a Vacation

evilly. "So we're going to leave you on that little island!"

The kids gulped. They knew the tide would soon cover the reef, and several ominous triangular fins slicing through the surrounding waters hinted that their "vacation" might be a very short one!

It was time for some fast thinking. "Oh, thank you, sir!" said Huey. "We'll have a real keen time looking for pearls and stuff."

"B-But—" began Donald.

"Have a good time, Gladstone!"

Dangerous Waters

broke in Dewey. "And don't forget to take your lucky pills! You know what happens if you don't!" He gave Gladstone a sneaky wink.

"Huh?" said Gladstone, puzzled.

"You know, your *lucky pills!*" repeated Dewey.

"Oh, sure, my lucky pills," said Gladstone hesitatingly, not quite catching on to what the kids meant, but going along with the gag, anyway.

Then Feisty spoke up. "What's this jazz about lucky pills?" he

A Little Reminder

demanded. "What'll happen if he doesn't take them?"

"Oh, nothing serious," replied Huey innocently. "He just loses his luck, that's all."

"LOSES HIS LUCK? Wh-what do you mean?" spluttered Feisty.

Huey explained that Gladstone's luck depended on taking special pills concocted from powdered pearls and a rare seaweed. He went on to say that only they, the kids, knew how to identify the seaweed, and only their Unca Donald knew

"LOSES HIS LUCK?"

how to prepare the pills.

Feisty and Turtleneck looked at each other. Were the kids pulling their legs? They decided to play it safe and take the ducks aboard.

"We can use a few extra hands!" said Turtleneck. The kids were to gather the seaweed, the crooks would supply the pearls from their loot, and Donald would make the pills and do all the cooking.

And Gladstone? Well, he was an extra-special passenger, and he would be treated accordingly—

A Big Decision

with the best cabin and food the schooner had to offer.

Gladstone liked the setup. Donald had other ideas, however, and later, in their cramped quarters, he let the kids know how he felt.

"Me cook for Gladstone?" he complained. "Why couldn't you kids dream up a better idea than that?"

His nephews patiently explained that it was their only chance to stay healthy while they figured out a way to escape.

Cooking Up Ideas

"I hope so," grumbled Donald. "I'd almost as soon take my chances with the sharks as pamper that mooching cousin of mine."

While Donald sulked and the kids planned their escape, Feisty and Turtleneck were burning the midnight oil in their cabin making some plans of their own.

Planning an Escape

Toasting the Skipper

CHAPTER 6

BREAKFAST IN BED

"With that Gander's luck and my great-great-grandpappy Blowhard's schooner, we are going to revive buccaneering's golden age!" declared Feisty. He raised a glass of kelp juice in a toast to a picture of a bearded, evil-looking sailor.

"We should have better luck than he did," said Turtleneck, hoisting his glass, too. "Remember, he had to retire to Patagonia after his last caper."

"Oh, well, anybody could mistake a camouflaged battleship for a pleasure yacht," explained Feisty. "He was just a bit nearsighted, that's all." He downed the kelp juice and wiped away a tear. "I'm going to make him proud of me, up there on that big desert island in the sky!"

Sad Memories

Their lamp burned far into the night as they made grandiose plans for the revival of big-time piracy. They would get a bigger and faster ship with the proceeds of their first job. Later they could acquire a whole fleet of raiders to scourge the seven seas!

With these plans swimming in their heads, the two ambitious buccaneers turned in, to dream of wealth and fame.

At the crack of dawn the next morning Feisty and Turtleneck set

The Future Looks Bright

sail for the open sea. The kids had dredged up some seaweed for a grouchy Donald to grind up together with a small pearl which Turtleneck had grudgingly donated.

They were well out to sea, going at a fast clip before a spanking breeze, when Gladstone appeared on deck, yawning.

"Sleep well, Gladstone?" asked Huey.

"Like a top!" replied Gladstone. "What's for breakfast?"

"Sleep Well, Gladstone?"

"Breakfast!" exclaimed Donald, poking his head out of the galley porthole. "We ate breakfast *hours* ago!"

"Oh, well, make it brunch then." His cousin shrugged. "I'll start with a glass of freshly squeezed orange juice, and then some eggs over easy, with a small breakfast steak, medium rare, and—"

"Hold it!" shouted Donald furiously. "What do you think this is, a luxury liner? You'll take flapjacks and *like* 'em!"

"Breakfast!"

"Flapjacks?" snorted Gladstone. "You know my delicate stomach can't tolerate such uncouth fare!" He was beginning to take seriously his role as a privileged passenger.

"Delicate stomach, haw," scoffed Donald. "I've seen you clean out my refrigerator at one sitting!"

Just then Feisty and Turtleneck appeared on deck. "What's all the fuss about?" asked Turtleneck.

"The cook won't give me what I want for breakfast!" complained Gladstone. "I can't feel very lucky

Gladstone Complains

on an empty stomach!"

"Give him what he wants!"
Feisty ordered the reluctant cook.
Donald obliged, not wishing to
face a charge of mutiny.

And so it went. Gladstone began
to act as if he owned the ship, and
Donald had to work harder and
harder to please his finicky tastes.

Gladstone was even beginning to
get on the would-be pirates' nerves
with his demands. He griped about
the mattress, the view from his
porthole, the color of his cabin, and

Giving Him What He Wants

the creaking of the rigging.

Feisty and Turtleneck grudgingly put up with this, not wanting to take a chance on his luck going sour. So the pampering and coddling went on until one morning when Huey came into the galley.

"I've got Gladstone's breakfast order, Unca Donald," he told the overworked cook.

"Why can't he give it himself?" growled Donald.

"Because he's in bed!"

"Is he sick?"

An Overworked Cook

Huey hesitated. "Uh, no. He wants his breakfast in bed!"

Donald turned the color of a boiled lobster and hit the ceiling. "He'll *get* his breakfast in bed," he yelled. "Right in the face!"

He grabbed a bowl of pancake batter and headed for Gladstone's cabin.

"Wait," cautioned Huey. "Don't do anything rash."

"Rash, shmash!" gritted Donald. "I've had enough of—"

He never finished, for as he tore

"Don't Do Anything Rash."

around a corner he collided with
Feisty and Turtleneck. Batter spattered all over the startled pirates.

"Wha . . . ptooey!" they spluttered as they wiped off the goo.

Turtleneck, recovering himself,
grabbed Donald by the neck. "Why
don't you look where you're going?"
he yelled furiously. "What are you
doing out of your galley?"

Donald managed to stammer an
apology. Just then Gladstone came
out of his cabin, scowling.

"Hey, knock off the noise!" he

Spattered Batter

demanded. "I'm trying to relax!"

"Relax, shmelax!" roared Feisty, grabbing him by the neck. "That does it! I've had it up to here with all this namby-pambiness!"

"Take it easy," broke in Turtleneck anxiously. "We need his luck, don't forget."

"Who needs his luck?" snapped the other. "Look!" He pointed up at the top of a mast. An albatross was just landing.

"An albatross!" exclaimed Turtleneck.

"An Albatross!"

"We Don't Need These Ducks!"

CHAPTER 7

PIRATES' LUCK

"Yeah, and you know that means good luck to sailors!" said Feisty triumphantly. "Now we don't need these pesky ducks anymore!"

The kids exchanged worried looks. "Gosh, Mr. Feisty," Huey said. "We can be awfully useful on board."

"Sure!" put in Dewey eagerly. "We can swab decks and pump the bilge and scrape barnacles."

"And sew sails and polish brass and everything," added Louie.

"Tell you what," mused Feisty after a moment's thought. "You kids can stay, but these other two swabs have to go overboard. I'm awfully sick of your uncle's cooking, anyway."

He and Turtleneck moved over to the rail, still holding Gladstone and Donald by their necks.

Trouble Ahead

"Have a nice swim, boys!" Feisty grinned evilly. "With luck, you can make it to shore in a couple of days!"

They were about to drop the two luckless cousins overboard when, with a splintering *crrrack!* the mainmast crashed to the deck in a tangle of ducks, pirates, and rigging.

The albatross flapped off, and, after some confusion, the ducks and pirates freed themselves.

Gladstone, who quite naturally

Saved By a Falling Mast

managed to avoid the mess, looked
over the scene calmly.

"Who needs whose luck now?"
he said smugly. "Let's see . . . where
were we before that unlucky albatross interrupted? Oh, yes! My
breakfast! I'd like a steak smothered in mushrooms, a tossed green
salad, and the rest I leave to your
nimble imagination, my dear cousin
Donald!"

"I'd like to smother you in toad-
stools," muttered Donald.

Feisty and Turtleneck looked at

Cross Words From Donald

each other and shrugged helplessly.
Gladstone had them over a barrel,
and they knew it.

"How about it, cook?" said
Feisty with a sigh. "Can you fix
him up?"

"We're fresh out of steak, and
we don't have any mushrooms," the
irate cook snapped. "He'll have to
settle for flounder smothered in
barnacles and a tossed kelp salad!"

But Gladstone wasn't about to
agree to that. "Go back to shore
and get what I want!" he ordered.

"How About It, Cook?"

"No steak, no luck!"

The pirates pleaded with him to be reasonable. They offered such delectable seafood substitutes as filet of stingray, shark scallopini, and squid casserole—but to no avail. Gladstone stubbornly held out for steak. The pirates, however, were determined he wouldn't get it.

It looked as if they were getting nowhere fast when Huey's sharp eyes spotted something appearing on the horizon.

Pleading Pirates

"Look!" he exclaimed. "There's a big boat over there!"

Feisty grabbed a spyglass and scanned the horizon. Sure enough, it was a big luxury liner.

"Maybe they'll lend us a steak," spoke up Dewey.

"Great idea!" exclaimed Feisty. "They live pretty high on those cruise ships. We'll flag 'em down. I hereby promise Gladstone here the best meal he ever ate!"

"Okay, but make it snappy," said Gladstone, yawning. "I think I'll

Approaching Liner

take a li'l nap meanwhile."

He returned to his cabin, and the pirates ordered Donald and the kids back to the galley.

"A steak is not all we're going to borrow from that ship!" Feisty remarked to his comrade in crime as they prepared to run up a signal flag.

"You mean—" began Turtleneck.

"Right!" replied Feisty. "We're going to take over the whole ship!" He hauled up a yellow distress

Comrades In Crime

flag. "Yes, sir, Grandpappy will be proud of us!"

Of course, with one mast down, the schooner wasn't making much progress, and it looked as if the liner might go by without noticing the distress signal.

While the pirates were wondering what else to do to attract the big ship's attention, Donald and the boys busied themselves in the galley.

"When is some of Gladstone's luck going to get us out of this

A Busy Crew

mess?" Donald grumbled as he struck a match and lit the old whale oil stove.

"Oh, ho!" chortled Huey, tossing some garbage out the porthole. "You *do* believe in Gladstone's luck!"

"I didn't say that," retorted his uncle angrily. "I only meant. . . ."

Just then the schooner gave a sudden lurch, spilling a big can of warm grease. It burst into flames as it hit the hot stove.

Trouble In the Galley

"Fire!"

CHAPTER 8

PIRATE PANIC

"Fire!" yelled Donald in panic.
He grabbed a bucket of water and
emptied it on the stove. Of course,
one doesn't put out a grease fire
with water, and all it did was to
spread the sputtering grease and
send up a choking cloud of steam
and smoke.

The kids knew better. They threw some baking soda on the blaze, which promptly extinguished it. Then they all went out on deck until the galley cleared of smoke.

Feisty and Turtleneck wanted to know what in blazes was going on. The boys assured them that all was under control, luckily.

"Luckily?" snarled Feisty. "You call that luck? You're going in the drink for sure now!"

The pirates made a grab for them, but they ducked under the

Nephews Help Out

pile of collapsed sail on the deck.

"Crawl under and chase 'em out!" Feisty ordered his pal, picking up a belaying pin. "I'll nail 'em with this!"

A mad chase began under the sail as the ducks scrambled around desperately to evade Turtleneck. They knew they were safe—for a short while, anyway—as long as they stayed under the sail.

Aboard the big luxury liner, the captain had just come out on the bridge after eating his noon meal.

"I'll Nail 'Em With This!"

"Anything new, Mr. Parkins?" he asked his first officer, who was scanning the horizon idly with his binoculars.

"No, sir," answered Parkins. "The same old dull, routine voyage."

The captain leaned on the rail and picked his teeth. "Y'know," he mused, "I almost wish we were back in the days of pirates. Then something exciting might happen. I get awfully tired of listening to gripes day in and day out."

Scanning the Horizon

Mr. Parkins suddenly stopped his scanning and peered hard at something. "Small craft to starboard, sir," he announced. "Looks like they might be in trouble!"

"What makes you think so?" the captain asked, grabbing the binoculars.

"Well, smoke's pouring out of a porthole, one mast is down, and they're flying a distress flag."

"You may be right!" the captain conceded as he stared through the binoculars. "Sound a general alarm

Spotting a Small Craft

and set an emergency course hard
to starboard."

Mr. Parkins quickly went into
action. The big ship made an abrupt
right-angle turn, adding a few
more little old ladies to the seasick
list.

Aboard the troubled schooner,
Feisty waited eagerly for a chance
to belt the first duck that showed
himself. He was oblivious to the
deep whistle blast of the approaching liner.

Turtleneck poked his head out

Waiting to Attack

from under the sail. "Hey, listen!"
he exclaimed. He got no further.
Whack! Feisty's belaying pin came
down hard on his noggin!

"Ouch! That smarted!" he
yelled, jumping out and holding his
head. "Since when do I look like a
duck, you numbskull?"

Another whistle blast came from
the liner. Feisty dropped his club.
"They're coming!" he shouted.
"Man battle stations!"

The two pirates hurried to an
ancient swivel cannon mounted in

"OUCH!"

the bow. "We'll fire a shot over their bow when they get in range," said Feisty. "It's loaded, and all you do is hold a match to the touch-hole when I say 'fire!' "

As the huge ship drew closer, the captain's voice boomed across the waves through a bullhorn. "Ahoy, *Bouncing Barnacle!* What's the trouble?"

"Fire!" shouted Feisty to Turtle-neck, who struck a match and held it to the firing hole of the old can-non to ignite the powder charge,

"It's Loaded!"

only to have the wind blow it out.

"Fire!" yelled Feisty again, this time at the top of his lungs. Turtleneck frantically lit one match after another. They all blew out.

Up on the liner's bridge, the captain turned to his first mate. "Break out the hoses," he ordered. "The schooner's on fire!"

In a very few moments powerful streams of water were drenching the schooner from stem to stern!

The pirates were rolled around

"Break Out the Hoses!"

on the deck, gasping and choking.

Crawling out from under the sail, the alert nephews were quick to size up the situation.

"Now's our chance to escape," cried Huey. "Let's get in that dory in the stern!"

They grabbed a slightly befuddled Donald and headed for the stern. At that moment Gladstone emerged from his cabin, blinking and looking around in confusion.

"C'mon, Gladstone!" cried the kids. "We're escaping!"

"We're Escaping!"

Gladstone hesitated. "B-But I haven't had my breakfast yet!"

A stream of water caught him and sent him spinning toward the stern, where the kids quickly hauled him into the dory.

"Lower away!" shouted Huey. In a jiffy they were in the water and rowing away from the schooner.

"Now turn your luck on," grunted Donald to his cousin as he hauled on the oars. "If we get out of this mess alive, I promise to cook

"Lower Away!"

you the best breakfast you ever ate in your life."

"Promises, promises," muttered Gladstone as he sulked in the dory's stern.

By now Feisty and Turtleneck had recovered themselves and abandoned all ideas about pirating the liner.

"After them!" screamed Feisty when he spotted the escaping ducks. "We'll run 'em down!" He grabbed the wheel and swung the schooner around.

Departing Ducks

"They're Closing In On Us!"

CHAPTER 9

PURSUED!

Feisty soon set a course directly for the dory. The schooner bore down on the ducks slowly and steadily.

"Faster, Unca Donald, faster!" cried Huey. "They're closing in on us."

"What do you think I am—a

steam engine?" gasped Donald, working the oars frantically. "Why doesn't my lucky cousin do something?"

"Oh, quit worrying," rebuked Gladstone irritably. "Something will turn up to get us out of this!"

The distance between the schooner and the dory narrowed rapidly, in spite of Donald's frantic zigzag maneuvering. They could see Turtleneck in the bow, grinning in evil anticipation of the coming collision.

Anticipating a Collision

Closer came the schooner, aided by the emergence of a stiff wind. It seemed that everything was going against the frantic fugitives. Through it all, however, Gladstone seemed strangely unconcerned.

The bow of the *Bouncing Barnacle* soon loomed directly astern, and the ducks closed their eyes and gritted their beaks, waiting helplessly for the awful crash that was only seconds away.

"Steady as you go, Feisty," hollered Turtleneck. "We've got 'em!"

Waiting for the Crash

But just as the crash appeared imminent, a sudden shift in the wind veered the schooner violently to one side. It jerked the wheel out of Feisty's hands and sent him sprawling to the deck.

He tried desperately to regain control of the wheel, only to get his hands whacked painfully by the wildly spinning spokes.

"Ow! Ow! Ow!" he yelled as the schooner jerked back and forth from port to starboard at the whim of the erratic wind.

"OW! OW! OW!"

But the troubles of the *Bouncing Barnacle* were only beginning. As the wind whipped it from side to side, a funnel-like form took shape from the bottom of a low, dark cloud hanging nearby. It touched down on the water and sent up a huge, whirling spray!

"Hey, fellas!" cried Gladstone, who had been watching this with great interest. "There's a waterspout! Open your eyes and watch the fun!"

The ducks stared in amazement

"There's a Waterspout!"

as the waterspout moved snakily toward the luckless schooner and hit it directly amidships.

With a great roar the waterspout twisted masts, sails, rigging, and pirates up into a gigantic braid. Then it dissipated as quickly as it had formed.

"See?" remarked Gladstone, cool as a cucumber. "I told you there was nothing to worry about. Now all we have to do is signal the liner and we're on our way home."

However, for once Gladstone's

A Luckless Schooner

luck seemed to have gone bad. The
liner was already a long way off,
and there was nothing to signal it
with.

On top of that, the dory seemed
to be caught in a powerful current
that was carrying the ducks swiftly
toward a dark mass of sheer cliffs
looming on the horizon.

The rock mass appeared to be a
volcanic island jutting out of the
ocean. "That's all we need!" Donald gasped as he struggled with the
oars. "A volcano."

A Rocky Mass Appears

"Don't worry, Unca Donald!" Huey tried to sound reassuring. "That volcano has probably been dead for a million years!"

"It's that 'probably' that I'm worried about," returned Donald.

Dewey squinted at the island. "Actually, the thing we do have to worry about is getting smashed on the sheer cliffs by the waves," he announced helpfully.

"Thanks a lot," mumbled Donald as he tried desperately to turn the dory around. But he couldn't

A Desperate Donald

pull it out of the current's grip.
"Grab an oar, Mr. Gander," he
told his calm cousin angrily. "It's
going to take more than your luck
to get us out of this!"

If Gladstone's faith in his luck
had been shaken, he didn't show it.
"Why strain myself?" he replied
with exasperating indifference.
"I'm just going to sit back and en-
joy the ride."

The kids had to restrain Donald
from whacking his cool cousin with
an oar.

Warding Off a Fight

"Cool it, Unca Donald!" begged Huey. "We're all in the same boat. Whatever happens to us will happen to Gladstone, too!"

"I wouldn't count on it," Donald retorted, eyeing a small, rocky reef nearby. "I think we should abandon ship and take our chances on that reef over there."

A faint roar from the direction of the island drifted to their ears.

"Hear those breakers?" Donald cried. "We'll be smashed to bits. All ashore that's going ashore!"

"Hear Those Breakers?"

With that, he prepared to dive overboard. The kids grabbed him, however. "Wait, Unca Donald!" they cautioned. "There's a big shark out there!"

They pointed to a menacing, triangular fin slowly circling the reef. Donald balanced on the edge of the dory, waving his arms wildly. Then, with a yell, he toppled into the water!

He came to the surface gasping and spluttering, and, in his confused state, he began to swim

"Wait, Unca Donald!"

frantically away from the dory.

"This way, Unca Donald!" yelled
the kids, trying to swing the dory
around. They had no success, however, as their frantic efforts only
tangled the oars.

The shark quickly became aware
of Donald's plight, and the big fin
zeroed in on the hapless duck. The
passengers in the dory watched in
helpless horror.

The Shark Zeros In

A Doomed Duck

CHAPTER 10

WHIRLPOOL!

"Good luck, cousin," called Gladstone with a choke in his voice as the dory drifted off out of sight around a cliff.

The shark circled around Donald, who yelled and thrashed the water wildly in a pathetically futile effort to drive him away.

Then, tiring of the game, the huge duck-eater reared up and moved in for the kill.

Suddenly one of Donald's hands closed around a piece of floating driftwood the size of a baseball bat. In sheer desperation he jammed it between the shark's gaping jaws just as the razor-sharp teeth were about to close on him!

The frustrated shark thrashed around trying to loosen the stick. It held tight, however, and Donald, with his last ounce of strength,

Angry Jaws Are Locked

made it to the reef and crawled onto it, utterly exhausted.

Meanwhile the dory, with its grieving passengers, was carried farther in the grip of the current toward the dark cliffs looming up ahead.

Nobody said a word; even Gladstone remained glum. They were too preoccupied with Donald's fate to notice that the apparently solid cliff face ahead actually contained a steep, narrow channel into which the current was sweeping them.

A Frustrated Shark

A faint roar broke them out of their unhappy meditating.

"Listen!" cried Louie. "What's that?"

"The breakers crashing on the cliffs?" suggested Dewey.

"No," gasped Huey in wide-eyed alarm. "You know what that is? It's the Whirlpool of No Return!"

They stared at each other, unable to speak. They had heard of this fearsome nautical phenomenon which pulled sailors to their doom in its swirling depths!

"Listen! What's That?"

The roar grew louder as they entered the channel and moved deeper between the forbidding cliffs. When the sound increased to the roar of a thousand jets, the channel widened at a point where two opposing currents met to form a wide, funnel-shaped depression in the water. It was the Whirlpool of No Return!

The dory was swiftly pulled into the swirling bowl. As the whirlpool opened up, the little boat spun round and round, faster and faster,

Whirlpool of No Return

like a ride in a nightmare amuse-
ment park.

Too dizzy to think, the terrified
nephews closed their eyes and hung
on for dear life. Even cool cousin
Gladstone began to have some faint
doubts about his luck.

As the whirlpool widened and
deepened, it exposed the bottom of
the channel, revealing wreckage of
luckless boats trapped long ago.

The dory ended its wild descent
as it skidded to a crunching stop
on the wet sand. Its passengers

A Rough Landing

climbed out shakily and tried to collect their swirling senses.

"Wow!" shouted Huey over the roar. "I'll never ride a merry-go-round again as long as I live."

He inspected the dory. Luckily, it appeared undamaged. "Our only hope now is that when the whirlpool closes in, it'll pick us up and float us to the top," he said.

His brothers nodded agreement and crossed their fingers. Then they got back into the dory to wait for the whirlpool to subside—all

"WOW!"

except Gladstone, who was gazing curiously at the wreck of an old ship.

"Better get in!" shouted Huey. "The whirlpool is going to close in any second!"

Gladstone didn't answer. Instead, he disappeared into the wreckage. Minutes passed and there was no sign of Gladstone. The water continued to creep toward the dory.

"Poor Gladstone," moaned Louie. "He's really pressed his luck a bit

"Better Get In!"

too far this time!"

The water was now deep enough to float the dory, and the boat slowly started to circle again in the vortex of the whirlpool. Suddenly Gladstone appeared out of the wreck, dragging a large chest.

"Get in! Get in!" screamed the kids. Gladstone shook his head and pointed to the chest.

"He wants us to take the chest!" yelled Louie. He jumped out of the dory and sloshed toward Gladstone. Dewey followed suit, and each of

Gladstone Finds a Treasure

them grabbed an end of the chest
and swung it aboard the dory as
it made one of its passes. It was
Gladstone's turn to get aboard as
the dory came around again. On
its third pass, the two kids climbed
aboard.

The whirlpool gradually dimin-
ished, and after a while the dory
was circling slowly on the surface
in an unearthly calm.

"Whew!" breathed Huey. "That
was too close!"

His brothers emphatically

"That Was Too Close!"

agreed. Gladstone only smiled.

"Shucks," he said with his old cockiness. "I wasn't worried!"

The kids exchanged skeptical glances. Then Huey asked, "What's in the chest, Gladstone?"

"Frankly, I don't know," replied Gladstone, fumbling with the lock. "I just had a feeling there might be something valuable in it."

The kids saw no reason to doubt him. Their thoughts turned sadly to Donald as they bent their backs and began to pull on the oars.

"What's In the Chest, Gladstone?"

"Poor Unca Donald!" sighed Huey. "I wonder what happened to him."

No one answered. They all tried manfully to suppress their sobs while wiping away their tears.

At that precise moment, an exhausted, castaway duck on a lonely reef was having similar thoughts.

"Poor kids! Poor Gladstone, too!" moaned Donald, sniffling and wiping away a tear. "I wonder what happened to them."

He was answered only by the

"Poor Unca Donald!"

waves lapping on the reef and the
sighing of the wind. He stared
despondently at the gathering
gloom, then lay down on the damp
rock and closed his eyes. He hoped
it was all a bad dream.

He had no idea how long he lay
there. Suddenly through his stupor
he heard a voice. "Hey, cuz! Can
we give you a lift?"

Donald didn't stir. "Wow, I'm in
bad shape," he thought to himself.
"I could have sworn I heard Gladstone offering me a lift. I must be

In Bad Shape

having hallucinations."

But a moment later he knew that
a whack on the back was no hallu-
cination. He looked up to see Gladstone standing over him. At the
reef's edge was the dory containing
his grinning nephews.

"Hop in, cuz!" said Gladstone
cheerily. "If you don't mind that
old treasure chest to sit on!"

Donald stared as Huey lifted the
lid to reveal the glint of gold coins.
He scrambled aboard, and soon
they were rowing toward home.

"Hop In, Cuz!"

"Well," said Huey, "we've got a hundred miles of shark-infested seas ahead of us."

"Without any food or water," put in Dewey.

"In a leaky boat," added Louie.

Donald looked at them and smiled. "For some reason, I couldn't be less worried!"

Gladstone said nothing; he just looked wise. Huey whispered to his brothers, "And *you* know something? I think there's another *believer* in this boat!"

Homeward Bound

Other **BIG LITTLE BOOKS**® Available

---

*With "FLIP-IT" cartoons

WHITMAN® Classics

Books for Your Permanent Library

BLACK BEAUTY

LITTLE WOMEN

HEIDI

HEIDI GROWS UP

TOM SAWYER

HUCKLEBERRY FINN

THE CALL OF THE WILD

TREASURE ISLAND

ALICE IN WONDERLAND

THE WONDERFUL WIZARD OF OZ

FAMOUS FAIRY TALES

ALGONQUIN

TALES OF POE

WHITMAN® *Full-Length Adventures*

Sports Stories
>   **CELLAR TEAM** (baseball)
>   **BASKET FEVER** (basketball)
>   **PLAYERS' CHOICE** (football)
>   **DRAG STRIP DANGER** (racing)

Short Story Collections
>   **ADVENTURE CALLING** (outdoor stories)
>   **SHUDDERS** (ghost stories)
>   **GOLDEN PRIZE** (horse stories)
>   **THAT'S OUR CLEO!** (cat stories)
>   **WAY OUT** (science fiction stories)
>   **LIKE IT IS** (stories for girls)
>   **A BATCH OF THE BEST**
>   (stories for girls)